UGLY DUCKLING PRESSE :: DOSSIER

ISBN 978-1-937027-18-6

Distributed to the trade by
SPD / Small Press Distribution
spdbooks.org

First Edition, First Printing

Ugly Duckling Presse
The Old American Can Factory
232 Third Street #E-303
Brooklyn, NY 11215

Funded in part by a grant from
the National Endowment for the Arts

**NATIONAL
ENDOWMENT
FOR THE ARTS**

uglyducklingpresse.org

COMMENTARY

(A TALE)

Marcelle Sauvageot

Translated from the French by
CHRISTINE SCHWARTZ HARTLEY
& ANNA MOSCHOVAKIS

Introduction by
JENNIFER MOXLEY

A NOTE ON THE TITLE

This book has been published in France under various titles: *Commentaire* (1933, 1934, 1936, 1986), *Commentaire: récit d'un amour meurtri* (1997), and *Laissez-moi* (2004, 2005, 2009, 2012). Marcelle Sauvageot herself was uncertain what to call her manuscript, describing the text to her first editors simply as "a commentary," a description they retained as title. For this first translation of the book into English, we have elected to restore that original title, along with the subtitle "récit" (a tale).

IL NE FAUT PAS ÊTRE ABSENT DE SON BONHEUR
WE MUST NOT BE ABSENT FROM OUR OWN HAPPINESS

Men cannot bear the gaze. In what Laura Mulvey described, in 1973, as the "active/passive hetero-sexual division of labour" that controls typical narrative structures, man is active and woman passive, because man "cannot bear the burden of sexual objectification." In 1933, forty years before these remarks, and three before Lacan would present his theory of the "mirror stage," it was just such an unbearable gaze that Marcelle Sauvageot turned on her former lover, her failed "double," when she published *Commentary*.

Throughout *Commentary* this lover remains, but for the endearment "Baby," nameless. But we see him. Not only sexually objectified but psychologically revealed. Hers is a gaze that penetrates deep into the psyche, past her lover's disingenuous utterances and awkward deceptions into the very heart of the patriarchal privilege that has made him a failed human being. From Sauvageot's perspective, neither his masculine entitlement nor his profession matter. She loves him. And love's happiness is complex. As Sauvageot elegantly defines it, love's happiness is not a knock out. It is, rather, a subtle intoxication. It allows us to reserve a "little corner of consciousness," that we might know we are in love. A corner from which we can spectate and appreciate the "slow evolution of joy," and say to ourselves, "I was happy, and I know why." For, in her existentially astute observation, "we must not be absent from our own happiness." This reserve, this "corner of consciousness," also enables us to see the other, free of love's blinding swoon. From it Baby's "weaknesses" and "insufficiencies" are visible. Is it so wrong if I love these as well, she asks him? But men, she realizes, want only to be admired. Once a woman says, "I love you," he will not judge her, but neither will he calmly abide that she retain that "corner of consciousness." She must find her happiness through him and for him. She must bear his gaze and be his mirror. Yet Sauvageot discerns that he is loath to become that same identity-instilling reflection for her: "But if you notice two eyes watching you, then smiling, you revolt. You feel that you have been 'seen' and you don't want to be seen: you want only 'to be.' Nervously, you ask: 'What are you thinking?'"

Sauvageot's pet name for her lover, "Baby," reminds us of Colette's sulky pretty boy and eponymous hero Chéri. In both *Chéri* and *Commentary* young men leave complex adult romances with strong independent women to marry, supposedly "out of obligation." In Colette's novel there is a large age difference between the lovers: Léa is forty-nine, Chéri twenty-five. Though nothing is explicitly said about Baby's age, there are hints. Sauvageot gives a breathless account of their rendezvous in Versailles at his "college," where his comrades, having checked her out, shoot him an approving glance. When she first meets Baby he is a "pale young man" with a determined look and lustrous hair dressed in dramatic black. He doesn't belong to any particular milieu, but seems ethereal, unperturbed by societal strictures. This is the Baby she loves, and this is the Baby she loses. He abandons his insularity and sweetness when he decides that in exchange for happiness he must live *comme il faut*, and to do so he must become, in her view, "mediocre." He sacrifices true love as soon as his concerns turn to "moral and societal principles." When thoughts of marriage enter his mind, his female lover—the forceful and independent woman whom he once saw as "rich with personal ideas"—is cast in a different light. Now she is rebellious and proud. Her once captivating ideas read as "egoism and demands." And, in the case of the strong-willed Sauvageot, this woman also happens to be dying.

It is an inconvenience. For Baby, her lover and addressee, "doesn't like the sick." Yet his discomfort cannot change the fact that tuberculosis is ravaging her lungs. When Sauvageot's tale opens she is on the train headed for her own Magic Mountain, a sanatorium in Hauteville, Switzerland. This is the fragile situation she is in when she receives a letter from her lover announcing his upcoming marriage to another woman. But, he assures her, their friendship "remains." This profoundly insensitive and cowardly letter triggers the writing of *Commentary*, which can be read as both a private journal and an epistolary response. Sauvageot exploits the intimacy of both forms to devastating effect.

Because of its private subject matter and intimate tone, it is significant that Sauvageot chose to publish *Commentary*, and thus to conduct her interrogation of heterosexual love in an open court. (We recall here that in Latin, *vulgare*, meaning "of the people" but also "to publish," was used as a slur against women who were thought to have made their bodies "public." Thus a vulgar woman is a woman who "publishes" that which men believe should stay private). Sauvageot was right to do so, for her concerns are the concerns of all men and women who have an investment in finding a way to respect each other and conduct their love affairs with honesty and equity. Those of us who, when desire brings us together across gender difference, will find, as Simone de Beauvoir put it, the "mutual recognition of free beings who confirm one another's freedom." What Charles Du Bos called, in his 1934 preface to the second edition of *Commentary*, "*l'amour de compréhension*,"—a knowing love—which is to say a love that is able to embrace the whole of who we have been, are, and shall become.

The scrutiny Sauvageot brings to her lover's shortcomings is no common plaint. Rather, it is an astute analysis of the disparity that exists between men and women when it comes to emotional accountability, a disparity fostered and supported by patriarchy. Yes, *Commentary* is a feminist work, but it is also an elegy: it is Sauvageot's lament for her love as well as for her life. One year after the publication of *Commentary*, Sauvageot will be dead of tuberculosis at the age of thirty-four. "Leave me," she writes in response to her lover's assurance of continued friendship, and then, more shockingly, "I want this erasure." Yet we all know how she feels. "Nothing will change between us, we can still be friends." What kind of craven self-regard allows us to utter such nonsense to our lovers? Both Sauvageot's furor and her resignation remind us of the voice H. D. gave the doubly aggrieved Eurydice. In H. D.'s poem bearing Eurydice's name she reproaches Orpheus for rousing her from death: "if you had let me wait / I had grown from listlessness / into peace, / if you had let me rest with the dead, / I had forgot you / and the past." Sauvageot's sanatorium bears an uncanny resemblance to Eurydice's underworld. There she grows listless into peace surrounded by "men and women in bathrobes, sunken-eyed," and "coughing." Her lover's letter amounts to one final backward glance. His motives for writing it are anxiety and guilt, as though, drawn forth by the light of the living, he hopes to settle his conscience before he leaves her and her illness behind. "If you love me, I will be cured," Sauvageot writes, almost as if to say, "you promised me I would live again and now I am condemned to a second death."

COMMENTARY

She does not recover. This we know. Du Bos would have us bathe her in the saintly light of *la petite fleur,* Saint Thérèse of Lisieux, who also died too young of tuberculosis. Perhaps Sauvageot did radiate an otherworldly peace as she met her end. Why should we doubt it? We must distinguish, however, how she ended her life with how she ended her book. *Commentary* leaves us not in the presence of an isolated woman in dialogue with her soul, but rather with a fully sensual, earthly being: a woman who, dreaming that she might find a truce with her illness, spends an evening at a ball. There, "the intelligent abandon that marries itself to the movements of another body" sweeps her ailing form into the dance—the happiest rhythm life knows. After this rapturous journey she leaves us, as does her nameless partner of an evening, at the threshold of our experience with a wordless kiss.

How lucky we are that this unique literary work, thanks to the excellent translation of Christine Schwartz Hartley and Anna Moschovakis, is available in English for the first time. Though eighty years have passed since its initial appearance, *Commentary* is a tale that still needs to be told. Though we may flatter ourselves into believing that we conduct our love affairs more maturely than did the barbarous moderns, even in these "enlightened" times readers will discover that Sauvageot's unsparing honesty about sexual love can still provoke deep recognition.

—Jennifer Moxley, Maine, 2013

COMMENTARY

7 November, 1930

"You take this as a proof of love, don't you?" The rhythm of the train scanned the sentence incessantly. I was cold; I was trying to sleep, balled up in a corner. —I was so cold!— Why had the train departed? The anxious feeling you get when doing something idiotic tightened in my throat; I had left a fragile happiness to return to the sanatorium; it was stupid. I'd experienced a bit of joy these past few weeks; surely, I was about to suffer a great sorrow in return.

"You take this as a proof of love, don't you?" Once again I could see the tormented face that had uttered this sentence to me the night before. And once again I could see, superimposed, the same face, so close to mine, eyes filled with heavy tears, that said: "Marry me, you will betray me..." If only I could have begun the scene again to kiss that face and say: "I will not betray you." But things do not begin again; and I must not have uttered that sentence, for I don't know how to speak at the right moment or with the appropriate tone. I am too easily overcome by emotion, and I harden myself to avoid giving in to it. How can one possibly convey the full sense of turmoil produced by an emotion at the precise moment it occurs? Let us fall asleep to this soft lullaby of a sentence: "You take this as a proof of love, don't you?" I am sending you a kiss through the air. If you love me, I will be cured.

And when I am cured, you'll see how everything will be fine. I like speaking familiarly to you now that you're no longer here. I'm not accustomed to it, it feels forbidden to me: it's marvelous. Do you think one day I will really be able to speak to you this way? When I am cured, you will no longer find me bad-tempered. I am sick. You told me the sick force themselves to be sweeter to those around them: and you cited some beautiful examples for me. I do not love you when you are delivering sermons; you make me want to yawn, and if you reproach me, it means you love me less: you're comparing me to others. The sick are sweet, but what I am is exhausted; carrying on and saying "thank you" to those who do not understand is wearing away all my strength. But you, what would you have needed a "thank you" for? You didn't understand because you don't know. I asked you what kind of mood you'd be in if, for a mere eight days, you were unable to sleep. In reply you said such things never happen to you, but that it had to be unpleasant. Of course you don't understand. In any case, I know: when we were in the country, you weren't happy; you wished you were in Paris, where your friend was. So you were in a hurry to get back and found me annoying. You see, this was another thing that turned against my desires: I thought my asking you to come would make you happy. You are much kinder in Paris...

and you find me much kinder: she is there. And then, you don't like the sick. I believe you'd be of a mind to have them locked up, eliminated. You should be sick.

"You take this as a proof of love, don't you?" What is one to make of this sentence? I know you no longer love me. It's comical, the care you take to avoid saying to me: "I love you"! You will have made me no promises. And yet it would be so good for me, alone, going far away, to cradle myself in your love with confidence. I need it: I would like to find it again when I return, cured. The certainty that someone continues to love and to wait, someone for whom all the rest is but a temporary, impotent distraction, is a great joy for the sick person: she feels the life she left behind has noticed her absence; she cannot imagine a brand-new future; weak and suffering from a brutal break with the past, what she asks of "later" is that it continue, and improve on, what came before.

I would like to keep the memory of last night like a talisman inside me. Let us close our eyes so the illusion can return. It's like

COMMENTARY

when you are dreaming: you must not move.
I love you.

Tenay-Hauteville!

I am afraid. I would like not to get off.

I would like to squeeze myself into a corner where people will not see me. I would
like to forget myself. How happy I would
be to keep traveling on this train, far away!
I waited in vain for a sign from fate: everything seemed to spur me to leave. What was
I to do? Now I must get off and go into that
sad house. But why must I? I sense in my legs

the almost voluptuous hesitation that makes you hold still when you have just one minute to take a decisive action. You say, "I will not move, I will not move…," and at the last second, with incredible speed, in a sort of mad panic, you commit the act you were hesitating to perform. I am brave; I got off; I completed all the paperwork methodically so as to prove to myself that I am strong. Someone in Paris loves me: I will be back. It's raining and foggy; four o'clock, the day is almost over. It would be nice at this hour to have tea with him, in a small and well-heated apartment. We would talk about when we were children. It's raining, and it's dark. I look intensely at the sanatorium to absorb in advance all the suffering I will experience there. Perhaps I will feel less pain. Men and women in dressing gowns, hollowed eyes, coughs; I can feel myself becoming sick again. Why did I come back? And in my bedroom, I sink into a chair; a heavy, pasty coat of boredom, sickness and despair presses down on my shoulders: I am cold. My beautiful dream leaves in pieces. I can no longer hear the voice, I am no longer enveloped in his love. When, in the morning, daybreak awakens us from a dream, we close our eyes and remain still, trying to recreate and prolong the scene. But the light of day has destroyed everything: words are without resonance, gestures without meaning. It's like a vanishing rainbow: some hues survive for an instant, disappear, seem to return: there is nothing left. This is how my beautiful dream disappears completely. Is it possible that nothing is left? Stupidly, I repeat: to get away from this place... and I try to recapture the pieces, to bring yesterday evening back to life. But it's a mirage; it breaks.

Tomorrow I will write to you and no longer know how to address you in this familiar way, I will write to you and will not know how to tell you everything I say to you in my heart. You who have remained there, among the living; can you understand that I am a prisoner? I no longer know how to speak. I am here, stupefied, and like a cold and certain truth I feel that, when one is here, nothing is possible anymore: you cannot keep loving me.

10 December, 1930

I have a lot of letters today: I will read his last. Perhaps it will say the things I am waiting for.

Since my return, his letters have disappointed and worried me: I truly believe he no longer loves me. I have been sick for two years, and often absent; he has kept on living; I wanted to believe he would wait for me; but in truth, was he waiting? Did things feel temporary and incomplete to him? Was he waiting for my return to make them blossom? Or were they dying with no regret on his part, certain as he was to find more beautiful things upon my return?

It's true that I am clumsy: I do not know how to express a feeling; by the time I've said a few words, I'm making fun of myself, making fun of the other person; with a single ironic sentence I destroy the impression I've created. It's a mistrust of myself; it's the surprise of hearing myself reveal what I feel, the way everyone else does. I listen to myself as if another person were speaking, and I no longer believe I am sincere; the words seem to inflate my feelings and turn them into strangers. And then I feel someone is going to smile the way one does at a child speaking of things of which she knows nothing. It can't possibly be me saying: I love you. What if someone believed me, and I had made a mistake! So I have to end my sentences with a pirouette that seems to say: "You, Sir, you love me, since you tell me so; but as for me, I'm afraid that loving the way I do may not be the proper way to love: others must know better than I how to love, must know better how to say it." I am afraid to discover one day that I do not love, and so I create doubt about my feelings in advance; I dread that I might come to be accused of insincerity; and so I imagine a thousand circumstances in which I presume my love will fail. I announce that I will not be faithful when in fact, to avoid displeasing, if only in thought, the one I've told I do not love, I turn down another man's offer to accompany me to the theater or kiss the tips of my fingers. And thus, in denying that my heart loves, I become more attached than the one who says to me: I love you.

I would like to be found out: but all people can see are the pirouettes and irony. He too must have seen only those; I did not show him anything else. Have I not asked too much of his waiting? And yet, these last few days, he has written me letters in which his jealousy pierced through. Surely, he must love me still. Perhaps this letter will be sweet.

"I am getting married... Our friendship remains..." I don't know what happened. I kept absolutely still and the room spun around me. In my side, where I hurt, perhaps a bit lower, I felt as if someone were slowly cutting my flesh with a very sharp knife. Everything underwent an abrupt change in value. It was like a movie that had become stuck, the un-screened frames of which would have projected only film without images; on the film that had already been viewed, the characters remained frozen in their poses like articulated dolls: they no longer held any meaning. They were filled with me and my expectation; I did not know what was going to happen to them, but I had lent them my soul; since nothing more takes place, all prior action empties out and breaks; I feel as though I have given my self over to an armature whose rigidity makes light of my anxiety: I cannot even blame it. The gestures initiated in the last exposed frame cause me pain; they were full of promises: the blank film keeps those promises.

When a form of suffering is unknown, we have more strength to resist it, for we are unaware of its power: all we see is the struggle, and we hope a fuller life will resume later. But when it is known, we wish we could cry for mercy with raised hands and say, in a tired stupor, "Again?" We foresee all the painful phases we will have to go through, and we know that what comes after is the void.

There will be the awakening at dawn, when the suffering is there, still powerless, and you pray to the Lord to let you sleep some more. It's like a tumor wrapped in cotton wool: and suddenly a violent stabbing pain makes itself felt. It's a small, precise image that two days earlier would have seemed harmless; it's a gesture, a glance tossed at another woman, barely noticed in the past, that, when pictured in the mind's eye, stops the heart with a painful spasm. It's a project devised in secret to please "him," the uselessness of which reveals itself in a brutal grimace. During the day or in the evening, there are moments of calm during which you are surprised not to be feeling anything; and you watch for the sentence, the sound, the perfume that will abruptly bring the pain back to life. The least little thing is a pretext for tears; a stupid sentence in the newspaper, which, on another day, would have elicited a shrug, now launches you into an abyss of emotion. And the other woman, what is she like? You endow her with every possible quality and see the two of them together, forever content with an extraordinary happiness; before the news, that happiness seemed insignificant. But now you are feeling very miserable and you feel like saying timidly: "I too could have made you happy; you told me so." You rebel, you curse, you wish for revenge. Revenge doesn't come or comes too late, when you have forgotten. It would be good right now, for it would allow whatever love remains in you to give itself and, perhaps, triumph. Our love doesn't have any power over "his heart" anymore. But if, suddenly, "he" were to suffer as we do because of the other; or, thinking it's too late, were "he" to miss us, then rushing over to comfort him would be a joy; in comforting the person who pushed it away, love comforts itself.

It is hard to think he no longer needs me.

Perhaps all this suffering is but a product of the imagination, which gives rise to concrete images and exaggerates feelings? Yet when I read, "I am getting married," although no image appeared, I hurt, I simply hurt, without any idea forming.

It was natural that you should tell me about your "friendship," all the purer for being free of desires, of jealousy, of expectation. We must give something; and so we think of friendship, "love's nobler sister," and we offer it while attempting to show how much better it is than the love we gave before, and now give to another.

You are quite persuasive; but then, one is never as persuasive as when in your position. Because one must first convince oneself, one discovers ingenious arguments and a warm tone with the most felicitous effect. And once the demonstration is over, one is so happy to have accomplished something that if the person being addressed is not convinced, it can only be because of her very bad temper.

Do you know what friendship is? Do you believe it to be a comparatively tepid feeling that contents itself with leftovers, and with the small favors that can't be avoided? Friendship, I believe, is a stronger and more exclusive form of love... but less "showy." Friendship knows jealousy, expectation, desire...

You were my friend, you wanted to marry me; this must have amounted to a lot of love...

And in the first letter I received from you a few days after my arrival at the sanatorium, you wrote: "I know you are seriously ill now. But it is certainly not out of devotion to another that you contracted this illness." Others, then, did not owe me anything because the rule of any friendship in the world, the rule of your friendship, was: "quid pro quo." I asked often; I did not always give: I was not to look elsewhere for the causes of what I took to be a loss of affection on your part.

You wrote me love letters, you wrote me jealous letters; you were unhappy for an entire evening because a friend remained between us for too long, and your last letter spoke of such suffering that you were unable to finish it. Then: "I am getting married... our friendship remains." I'm not saying that you were putting on an act: only that it took more than one day for you to stop loving me.

You called me your "gal"; I was the one who was supposed to know everything, and you were the one who was supposed to listen to everything. But you said nothing. Don't tell me it's my fault and that I should have interrogated you. A friend doesn't need to be questioned in order to confide.

Our friendship will be a very pretty thing in the future; we will send each other post-cards from our travels and chocolate bonbons at New Year's. We will visit each other; we'll tell each other of our projects the moment they come to fruition, in order to hurt each other just a little, and to avoid enduring any commiseration in case of failure; we will pretend to be who we believe ourselves to be and not who we are; we will say "thank you" and "excuse me," the kind words people say without thinking. We will be friends. Do you think it's necessary?

14 December, 1930

Some ballads begin as your letter does: "You, whom I loved so much..." This past tense, with the present still resounding so close, is as sad as the ends of parties, when the lights are turned off and you remain alone, watching the couples go off into the dark streets. It's over: nothing else is to be expected, and yet you stay there indefinitely, knowing that nothing more will happen. You have notes like a guitar's; at times, like a chorus that repeats: "I could not have given you happiness." It's an old song from long ago, like a dried flower... Does the past become an old thing so quickly?

Happiness? It's a term of complaint. You— you embodied it, you identifed it, you define it. Can one really speak about it as you do?

When you like a perfume, you try to hang on to it, to find it again; you don't let yourself become completely intoxicated by it, so you can analyze and soak it up little by little, until the mere memory of it can produce the same physical sensation; when the perfume returns, you inhale it more slowly, more softly, in order to perceive its most tenuous emanations. A brutal whiff of perfume makes your head spin but leaves an irritatingly incomplete, unfinished sensation. Either it's an unpleasant, suffocating feeling you'd like to be rid of so you can breathe freely, or it's a brutal intoxication, over too soon because only the nervous system has been touched. To be turned upside down and no longer know anything—that is happiness. But to hang on to a little corner of consciousness that is always aware of what is happening and that, because it is aware, can allow the intellectual and rational being to also enjoy, fully, with each passing second, something of the happiness that arises—to hang on to this little corner of consciousness that appreciates the slow evolution of joy, that follows it to its farthest reaches, isn't that happiness? There's a little corner that does not stir, but that remains witness to the joy being felt; that remembers and can say: I was happy, and I know why. I don't mind losing my head, but I want to capture the moment when I lose it, to push my understanding of my abdicating consciousness as far as it can go. We must not be absent from our own happiness.

This corner of myself judged you, measured you; and in judging and measuring you I saw your weaknesses, your insufficiencies; where is the harm in my staying, in my accepting these insufficiencies, in my loving them? O, Man! You always want to be admired. *You* do not judge, you do not measure the woman you love. You are there, you take her; you take your happiness, she seems not to belong to herself anymore, to have lost all sense of anything: you are happy. To you she cried:

I love you, and you are satisfied. You are not brutal; you are gentle, you talk to her, you worry about her; you comfort her with tender words; you cradle her in your arms. But you do not judge her, since you are asking her to be happy through you and to tell you that she is happy through you. But if you notice two eyes watching you, then smiling, you revolt. You feel that you have been "seen" and you don't want to be seen: you want only "to be." Nervously, you ask: "What are you thinking?"

I am thinking about you. You have a small, throaty laugh and teeth I do not like. Your eyes close slightly, as if to penetrate the mind of the person you're speaking with and show him that you have seen clear into him. Your lips recede somewhat over teeth that appear black, and your whole head strains forward. You assume this air when you are expounding a brilliant theory you have just discovered, or when you have found a way to reduce what someone had believed to be a beautiful thought to a mediocre sentiment. You look like a shopkeeper who won't be pushed around. I am embarrassed when you are like this: it diminishes you. But no one had better take notice of this minor flaw and say something: I would be very mean. You have odd judgments sometimes, in fields you claim to know nothing about. You take down a painting, a piece of music, a poem with your words: it's facile. It's as if you want to recover your stability, compromised for a moment by something greater than you; and you are so afraid of snobbism that you reject what you have experienced as beautiful. I see it, and I don't like it. But were others to intimate any doubts as to your taste and your intelligence, I would reply sharply, as if I were being insulted. You are a bit vain: you steal satisfied glances at yourself in mirrors on the sly, you straighten up when passing by a woman, and you stare at her while maintaining an attitude of false indifference; if she glanced at you, surely she found you handsome; if someone tells you about a woman, you interrupt to ask: "Is she pretty?" I find you amusing, and I feel like smiling derisively. But let no one tell me you're a "ladies' man"; your weaknesses are my own. I discovered them little by little, by examining you without rest. I suffer from these faults of yours, but I wouldn't want you to change. I sometimes talk to

you about them, smiling. I wouldn't want
to offend you, or to give you advice. I would
like for you to know what I know; and I wish
that instead of trying not to show yourself as
you are, you would reveal all your little ugli-
nesses to me. I would love them, because they
would truly be mine. Other people wouldn't
know about them; and this is how we would
find each other outside this world. Nothing is
more endearing than weaknesses and faults:
it is through them that one penetrates the
beloved's soul, a soul perpetually concealed
by the desire to seem like everybody else. It's
the same as with a face. Others see only a
face; but *we* know the precise moment when,
instead of continuing along its ideal line, the
curve of the nose breaks imperceptibly to
delineate an ordinary nose; we know that, up
close, the texture of the skin is coarse, with
blackheads; we have discovered the blemish
in the eye that sometimes dims the gaze, and
the extra millimeter that keeps the lip from
being elegant. These small irregularities, we
feel like kissing them more than the per-
fections, because they are humble, and they
make this face not be that of another man.

Do not complain that I am judging you and measuring you: I know you better, and that is not to love you less. It was not I who was unhappy, but you. You should have rephrased the sentence in your letter to say: "You know quite well that you could not possibly have given me happiness, because even in the moments when we were closest, you always withheld a corner of yourself... that did not stir... that was judging me."

For that matter, was it you I was judging, or myself? You know full well that I am always watching myself as I live, that I make fun of myself, that I belittle myself, that I laugh at my impulses and my enthusiasms, that I deny myself any self-confidence. So I had no confidence in you either. I wasn't sure, despite all your love. You had many woman friends: I did not reproach you for this; I would have liked for you to tell me about them, so I could know what drew you toward them, away from me. But you told me very little. I thought you did not love me and didn't dare question you, when I wanted so much to know. I worry over a glance, a word, a silence ... but I say, "You are free," because I don't want a person to stay out of obligation and I would like for him to stay nonetheless. The thing is, I understand so well when someone does not love me anymore that I find any effort to fight or hold on foolish. Such effort would be so pointless, I laugh at my least inclination to protest: "You, jealous? Oh no! That isn't your style: don't say anything. All you would elicit is a smile, a few painful words of appeasement... And he would leave anyway, just as fast, not any faster... So: you are free."

I tried to hold onto a small support separate from you, so I could cling to it the day you would no longer love me. This small support was not another man, it was not a dream, nor an image. It was what you called my egoism and my pride; it was my self that, in my suffering, I wanted to be able to find again. I wanted to be able to hold myself tight, alone with my pain, my doubts, my lack of faith. When I am in distress, only my sense of self gives me the strength to go on. When everything is changing, when everything is hurting me, I am me with myself. To have lost myself, I would have had to be sure I no longer needed myself.

You describe your fiancée in a periodic sentence whose rhythm conforms to the evolution of your feelings; it draws itself out slowly, tilting progressively toward its terminus, where it stops for good without a sound, lacking the strength to go further: it is there, stopped forever, just as you are there close to Her.

If I were very vain, I would think you still love me and that it is out of a sense of obligation to avoid injuring a young girl who

believes in you that you are distancing yourself from me to marry her. But rest assured:
I am not at all vain; I only smiled at a few
words: "compelled," "fear of disappointing
her." I also thought that if I were your fiancée
and if I read this sentence, I would be sad-
dened. I wouldn't like for a man to marry me
so as not to disappoint me; so as not to show
me who he is. This half-lie, as the basis of a
union, would offend me; I think I would pre-
fer to leave. But these are my own ideas. In any
case, your fiancée did not read the sentence:
she doesn't know "what you are." And if she
knew, she would probably be happy to have
such an homage paid to her love. Is a woman
in love not delighted when a man chooses her
as a reward for her total love? You enrich your
feelings with a confused and happy gratitude
for the contentment She is giving you, of
which you are not worthy and which you will
not be able to return. All this, with a touch of
superstition, sets "my teeth on edge" slightly;
I don't know why, because what you are saying is the eternally idiotic, but eternally true,
song of those who love and are loved. I am
not making fun. What you are saying in this
sentence, underneath all these words, is that

you love, and that you love a woman who is different from me, that you love her for all she is in opposition to me, that you have loved her for a long time without ever wanting to tell me.

Last year, in the country, the day after you arrived, we climbed the path halfway up the slope; sitting in the tall dry grasses, we were looking out at the prairie and I'd seated myself right next to you. Softly, I talked to you about your friend: you didn't answer. I insisted, and you said somewhat dryly that it was a part of you I didn't love and that you would rather not show it to me. Your gaze became distant; you made a gesture, with your hand, of someone who wouldn't be understood; then you looked at me with the superiority of one who will not speak. You talked about something else. I fell silent; a dark veil had fallen over the joy I'd felt on seeing you again. For six months, I had been sick, far from you. You hadn't forgotten me, but someone was making you see me differently from the way I was. You reproached me for my character, my tastes... You became partial to the things I disliked: I had the disorienting feeling that you were thinking about someone who was the absolute opposite of me and that you were making a constant comparison. You had a fixed idea of who I was; and in my words and gestures you were looking for anything that could be attributed, one way or another, to this idea. You credited me with petty feelings, a monstrous egoism, demands... And I gave up telling you that you were mistaken, because you had the self-assurance of a man who knows how to say "that's not true," and how to laugh with the kind of laughter that precludes all protest, because one gets the sense that nothing could puncture "his truth." You approved of what you had once found idiotic; you ruined what had seemed to be your most intimate thinking. It was as if you were trying to kill me inside of you. I was in pain; the faults you held against me and the qualities you acknowledged I had mattered little to me: you no longer wanted to see me as I was; and I wept to see myself destroyed in this manner.

You explained how you recognized the love of a woman "without prerogatives and without demands."

If you feel like spending an entire day spitting into the water to make rings, the woman who loves you will spend an entire day, without saying a thing, watching you make rings in the water: she will be happy because this pastime pleases you. And if you feel like making rings in the water every day, then this woman, every day, will stand there watching you do it. You added that I wouldn't be able to remain there like that. I feel compelled to confess that I would not. I would first attempt to sleep, or else do something myself; and, if that weren't possible, I would not be able to resist telling you that you're a fool and you'd be better off kissing me. Then I would come stand beside you to make rings in the water too, to do what you do, and I would invent the game of the biggest rings and the smallest. Would you really have been able to stand next to me watching me make rings in the water?

In Corsica, after a long walk through the scrub brush, I came upon an open path. I held my horse by its bridle; its head was above mine, and I was barely visible between two arbutuses: I was holding pink peonies against my breast. I wished you could have been there to smell the fragrance of the brush; you would have understood the taste I have for the wild sometimes; you would have been simple and wild like me and we'd have loved each other. I held my horse tightly in my arms and crushed the peonies. There was no one around to love what I loved.

On Venetian gondolas, at night, along the fetid canals where a raspy *Sole mio* is sung beneath tricolor lanterns, near the dead, sad palaces, I cried because I was alone and because I knew you wouldn't have let your-self be carried away with me by this morbid charm.

From the tops of mountains, gliding as in a dream down tall slopes covered in white snow, I thought to keep the marvelous vision in my heart, so that, back at your side, I could make you see it; I searched for words intense enough to make you taste my joy and give you the desire to come with me. But you quickly stopped listening to me and took on a somber look.

COMMENTARY

I wanted to take you to see dances and to hear special concerts. I did everything in my power to make you content, and my own happiness was greater when you were moved. But you resisted accompanying me, and you stopped wanting to come along.

Wherever I was, you were within me. You placed yourself in the way of my feelings. They were sad because you weren't there. I tried to preserve them in all their detail, to be able to bring them to you almost raw. Did you never sense the passion I put into trying to bring them to life for you? I thought about keeping you with me all the time so you could feel what I felt, so that nothing of my experience would occur in your absence: the glint of the sun in my eyes, the posture of my body in a dance… And I became impatient if I felt myself flourishing when you weren't there. A success satisfied me because I could tell you about it; a problem was alleviated because I could recount it to you. I wanted to do more things, always more things, in order to bring you the growing bounty of my enrichment.

And at night, in the streets of Paris where I always walked quickly without seeing anything, I tried to love what you loved. I timidly put my arm under yours like all the couples on the street, and, curious to feel what you felt, I liked the perfume of the fog, the brush of the crowd, the bustle of the shop girls. In the dark streets, athough I detest all public displays, I took pleasure—a forbidden pleasure—in returning your kisses, which weren't very "comfortable" but were sweet because you liked them. During hot summer afternoons on my bedroom sofa, we sang ballads, dance tunes from ten years back; the lyrics were silly and I am not sentimental; but next to you, whose soul is more romantic than mine, I let myself be swept away by the simple melodies, evocations of the masses who are moved and captivated by the crude song of human tenderness. The "tango of dreams, tango of love" helped me get a bit closer to you… I would have liked to read what you'd read and see what you'd seen. But you said only a few quick words, as if none of this was meant for me.

When people talked about love around me, I thought of yours, and I smiled: when they talked about "men" and the harm they cause "women," I kept on smiling, because I thought you weren't one of those "men."

But that wasn't loving you, because I still wanted to enrich myself, because I didn't want to destroy myself in order to become an acquiescent form with no desire left for self-improvement, that instead falls asleep in childish admiration of the man it loves and lets itself be guided by him.

It's curious how frequently a man, the moment he thinks about marrying the woman he has loved for a long time, becomes obsessed with moral and societal principles. This woman he loved because she was strong, independent, rich with personal ideas—when he thinks about marrying her, his instincts of domination and pride, and his preoccupation with "what people will say," transform strength into rebellion, independence into pride and bad temper, personal ideas into egoism and demands. He points out that life is made up of small daily incidents to which one must adapt and for which one must prepare by adopting an average "mentality." One ought to specify each party's role in advance, because this is no longer the time to act like children. Toward his wife the man will be respectful, loving; he will say in a soft voice that one should not go here or should not go there, that one should behave like this and not like that, because it's everyone's custom; the wife will say, "yes, my darling"; and when in the company of her friends, you will hear her lend her voice to the universal chorus that proudly repeats these words: "my husband." She pronounces the word with a delight imbued with arrogance, astonished as she is to now be among the elite who can say: "my husband." Each of them in turn outdoes the others with tales of what the "husband" does, what the "husband" says; all the loving gestures or reproaches made by "the husband" are revealed beatifically, like so many jewels brought as an offering to the young woman. With every question asked or subject broached, you are sure to hear: "I will ask my husband," or: "My husband told me…" As I write these lines, I can hear, on the terrace next to mine, a group of young and pretty women conversing with animation and good cheer. I cannot understand what they are saying; but I can clearly make out, as a constant and frequent refrain, "my husband"; when I come across them during a walk or at lunch, if I catch a few words of their conversation, these words are always: "my husband." Is it really necessary to become like this, and can a woman not think except with the husband's ideas? This might make you smile, lead you to think that resentment has made me sarcastic. But I am so bored with all these women who talk about their husbands!

Many a sentence in your letter aroused these "feminist" thoughts in me. Was it intentional that you didn't understand why I asked you to return my photographs? I am not so vain as to think that they would remind you of me and that this reminder would be a nuisance in your new life: daily life will quickly wear away the vividness of things past. Nor did I want to make the traditional gesture that lovers make when parting ways. I would gladly leave all these things from the past with you, because they no longer have any meaning or importance. The thing is, I thought about your wife. That you wouldn't tell her about me, I understand; but then you must not keep anything of mine in your house: it would be a cumbersome secret she might discover. If you tell her about me, I feel a certain unease thinking that it will perhaps be in the tone you used when telling me about other women you had loved. There is one about whom you said, to explain your breakup: "I'd had enough." Your eyes hardened; you spoke in a husky, hoarse voice, from deep in your throat, and for a moment your eyes became fixated on a point in the distance. This was a reason without chance of appeal; one says as much, upon leaving the table, when one has lunched well: it would be wrong to insist. A few seconds later, you rubbed your eyes for a long time, and added with a sigh that came from deep in your heart: "She is married: I sincerely wish her all the happiness in the world." I don't know why we ascribe any importance to what a lover will say about us later. Is it pride? We don't want to be treated like the others. So, for now, I would rather be able to tell myself that you will never speak about me. But there are my photographs, which your wife can find. You'll tell me that you will "handle" the pain this discovery may cause her. I wouldn't want you to "handle" it. That offends a certain, very deep feeling I have of feminine self-esteem. I imagine you will console her: you will be much more tender, more affectionate, more attentive; you will make her questions vanish under caresses: you will "make do." Don't you realize how humilating that might be, and the hatred it might spawn? I don't want you to have to "handle" this consolation because of me.

Why do you ask me: "Does he exist, the man you were made for?" People say to a woman: "The man you were made for," and to a man: "The woman who was made for you." Can they envision: "The woman you were made for"? A man is: everything seems to have been made available to him… even, somewhere in the world, a woman who suits him, whose union with him existed before her birth. These words—"you were made for"— imply an obedient and submissive adaptation on which a woman's happiness will depend. Strange thing: the woman is made for the man and it is she who will be made happy.

Can the man not be made happy, or does his happiness reside in feeling the consenting pliability of the one who is made for him? Is the man caressing a beautiful Siamese cat hoping to find out what the animal's light eyes are saying? Or does he think that the caress itself is the only thing that can cause the animal to be moved?

I find this idea of the pre-existence of a union very pretty. A Japanese legend, I believe, has it that at birth, the moon attaches the foot of a future man to the foot of a future woman with a red ribbon. While they are alive, the ribbon is invisible, but the two beings look for each other and, if they find each other, their happiness will be on earth. Some do not find each other; as a result their lives are restless and they die sad: for them, happiness will begin only in the other world; they will see the one to whom the ribbon attaches them. I don't know if I will find the red ribbon that is attaching me in this world; I think this legend is, like all legends, a poetic comfort. Isn't the man for whom you are made the man for whom you accept you have been made? That man, for me, could have been you.

I sense constantly in your letter the desire you have to mask the one and only truth it contains behind verbal argument, humility, subterfuge... almost. Some of it is amusing.

"Undoubtedly you were right, I know... but who knows what would have happened if you hadn't been?"

So ends your first sentence. I can't help but think of the old formulation: "What would happen if everyone did the same?" It's a question people ask when they no longer know what to say: because they simultaneously lift their eyes a little to take the heavens as their witness, they look as if they are making an argument of importance. If I had not been right not to trust, either I would eventually have trusted... or things would have continued as they were: I would not have trusted, you would have loved me still...

Why this humility? "I know that what I am writing might seem contradictory to you... not hold up."

I cannot find a single contradictory thing in the feelings you have just expressed. But you're the one who, thinking he has run out of arguments (while everything he has said is clear, definitive, indisputable) leans toward his interlocutor, stares at him intently, appeals to lofty sentiments and allows himself to appear illogical so that the other will acquiesce to his claims. Later, he will re-establish the order of things and deem himself logical. Please note, too, that in this scenario it is me you are accusing of being illogical. I would have to be afflicted with a bizarre sense of reasoning not to understand and to attempt to talk about my "ideas," when you're going on about feelings. But perhaps I'll just stop at the word "friendship" to note with a smile how frequently you now use it with me. When I timidly said "friendship," you replied with ardor: "love." Today if I display some of my love, you seem shocked and "do not for an instant doubt my current feelings."

This expression—"I do not for an instant doubt"—can concede to anything, since it suggests in advance that it doesn't matter anymore: the next words will be: "But... I regret..." Steadfast in a decision... or a line of reasoning, one can vouch with some force that one "does not for an instant doubt..." You scoured the past for a sentence in which I seemed to say I no longer loved you: "You always told me that what you had loved in me was 'Baby,' and you did not conceal from me that 'Baby' no longer existed." And you shield yourself with this sentence without wanting to remember how you did not accept it. Now, you welcome it with glee, because it enables you to escape reproach for your infidelity. I could, in turn, simply say: "You often told me that you would wait for me… You did not tell me that you weren't waiting for me anymore."

It's an art to be able to secure a retreat this way; and your "… and you didn't conceal from me" concurs felicitously with "I do not for an instant doubt": I see a petty salesman reneging on a deal he no longer wants to close.

"Baby" was a small, pale young man, dressed in black. He had beautiful blue-black hair and large glasses behind which small brown eyes peered insistently. They were meant to be insolent: in fact they were timid and gave themselves away. Baby didn't seem to belong to a "set." You would think he had sprung up here from outside any group. He held to many systems and theories; but they disappeared and were replaced quickly depending on the day: it was as if he hadn't held them. He had retained every prejudice there is, but he seemed not to ascribe them any value: he had hung onto them just so he could understand those who still abided by them and those who had overcome them.

He didn't know me and knew none of my friends: there was no image of me inside of him that I would have to respect; and, since he didn't belong to a "set," there was no model image of a woman inside him with which mine would collide. I immediately felt like talking to him about myself. I had been looking forever for someone for whom I could screen my movie. Doesn't every human being experience this weakness? I would talk to myself, but the austerity of the monologue wore me out sometimes; it is so much easier to have an accomplice who sympathizes, approves, listens; you gain in importance; the things you say become tangible, form a novelistic universe in which you assume a role. To what extent do you respect the absolute truth? Then these little novels are drained of their suffering: it settles, becomes an entity outside of the soul. From time to time, I needed this comfort. I stiffened to maintain my integrity; but, to assuage my suspicions, I thought by recounting my life I could relieve it of its anecdotal character: its arc would make itself visisble to me. I needed a double.

I found the young man dressed in black with eyes that gave themselves away attractive; I called him "Baby" and I talked to him every day. I methodically recounted every minute of my day to him, and from then on, when he wasn't there, it was to him I spoke in a whisper. Each thing would assume its full value and flavor only after I had exhibited it to him: not that I took him as a guide, but he was the point of departure for my actions and reactions. And I loved him as if he were me. I wanted to cherish him well; he was very precious to me, and I was afraid of losing him.

But, one day, I sensed that Baby no longer existed. He didn't have his black clothes anymore; he had joined a "milieu" and no longer understood the man who stood apart. If excited in any way, he would cry: "tallyho"; and his doctrine, now settled, was to live a mediocre life in order to be happy. He didn't want to follow me anymore. And my stories made him shrug his shoulders. Baby was dead and it was Baby I loved. But the person who remained resembled him so much that the illusion persisted, and I did not give up. You do not separate from your double in a few instants because he has suddenly disappeared. You chase his image, his memory; you hope you are mistaken; I thought he wasn't dead, that he would return later when I was better. Was it possible that he'd cast off everything I'd told him?

You found my influence "nefarious." Today you recall this influence and you find it a credit to our friendship. Why? The stories I told you, the influence I may have had on you, no longer exist. We have changed the tone of the two beings who kept them alive... And what hurts me is not so much the death of a love as that of a truly living being that the two of us created, that perhaps I created alone... This being was a union of you and me, as we wanted ourselves to be. It was you as I needed you to be, not as the admirer of my person that you claimed to be, but as a man who loved me; who, as a result of this love, found interest in everything that originated in me; in front of him, I was allowed all my faults and all my good qualities; I could let myself be a mess... the kind of lyrical, unexpected mess where every instinct is surrendered in words or cries so that later, the sure-handed steering of the soul can return it to its path to continue on. And I imagined that none of this abandon clouded your love or your trust.

And then there was, in this created being, the mysterious woman I was for you. I didn't know what life you found by my side: happiness, joy, anxiety, boredom... So many questions! I didn't answer them. At certain times, I thought I was indispensable, at others, an accident. I had moments of confidence and hours of sadness. And it was necessary for me not to know what I was for you, just as it was necessary for you not to know what you were for me. The spell between us was meant to last for as long as we held on to the anxiety created by our respective ignorance of our image in the other's eyes. Who broke that spell? We thought we had seen the fixed image the other had of us, and we fixed the other's image in ourselves. Is that what separated us?

Oh! Do not think I saw you then as a "stopgap." There's no use in humbling yourself again and calling yourself an "object." I cannot help thinking that it is out of false humility that you speak that way. A few months ago you thought you were getting close to the man I may have found attractive. You know that resignation is not one of my traits; I sometimes seem to be giving up, but I am always pondering some means by which I can "turn around" my renunciation. So, would I have consented to live with you out of resignation? The torment of loving does not push me to the point of looking for a stopgap; and if that really was what I was doing, I don't see why I would have thought of you; your defection, if I may say, would not hurt me as it seems to do; I would resign myself once again to taking another object. Isn't there inside you, even when you seem self-effacing, a rather precise little vanity that doesn't give up?

In my enthusiasms, in my choices, you see intentions I do not have. I think the poor results of my romantic diplomacy are proof that I do not often ask myself whether I am right to love. It is quite possible that you really may have been just a stopgap for me, but that isn't how I saw you. I was beginning to feel that you had taken on a special place for me. Yet your intelligence didn't understand me any better, perhaps less well; your love didn't prove itself more delicately; your dedication didn't shine more brightly; perhaps everything in you was mediocre. But I preferred whatever came from you. Why?

This preference you attributed only to the taste I had for loving you; and your attraction to me was the desire to conquer me. Whereas in the past, your love was "this desire to conquer me entirely" joined with a much larger proportion of dedication, affection, incessant thoughts... In short, joined with all those feelings that, combined, muddled, make up precisely what people call love. Now this love is made of one small element, the thinnest, the least able to produce: the "desire to conquer," which you inflated so it would fill everything with its emptiness. To love is, for one person, to conquer, for the other, to submit... and all the rest receives the vague terms of friendship, affection, devotion...? Should I doubt love or you? Fortunately, this was not in fact all there was between us; but whatever else there was, I called love.

During the sad month of October you allude to, I was destroyed by suffering caused by a man other than you. It was from you that, spontaneously and by choice, among many more qualified others, it seemed, I asked for the strength to forget and to laugh. I begged you to listen to me talk about the other; I missed him when you were here, I almost resented you for not being him. Your love, discreet and tenacious, disinterested, and perhaps heroic, prevailed over my stubbornness. Since you loved me that much, it was no longer possible for me to say, stupidly, that everything was hopeless.

And I felt a great deal of sweetness—a sweetness that indeed seemed to be that of love—in seeing you love me, and in remaining close to you. Do not analyze this memory: in it I can see only love.

As for me, I am not quite sure what feeling drove me to come see you in Versailles: love, the friendship of a man?... yes, it was all this, to which I did not give a name, but which caused in me the disorientation one generally sees in very young lovers. I was in Paris only one day a week; the main point of that day was to see you. To be with you for a quarter of an hour, I would use up my entire afternoon in a taxi that drove me to your "college." Overexcitement was the dominant note in me before I saw you; when I left you, it was the exhaustion that follows a long wait. I saw you between noon and one. I drank a little tea at eleven and lunched without hunger at two, because a ball was rising and falling in my throat. Taxis were too slow, "roadblocks" exhausting; at the Saint-Cloud station, I never knew which streetcar to take: I wanted to get on the first one; I ran to one, then to the other... and every time I turned my back, the one I had abandoned would be leaving. In my impatience, I would get off at the stop before the one I needed, and when I

resolved to be patient I let the overly anticipated stop go by. And so I would run, anxious
about being a few minutes late; then I'd stop
because I was twenty minutes early. I think
I always ended up being late. I'd bring you
chocolate bonbons. We would sit down in a
little dark room, on two hard chairs. There
was always a little Annamese man in a corner
waxing the floor. He didn't make any noise...
and all of a sudden we would notice him. He
inconvenienced us enormously. He would
look at us, dumb. Did he understand? Then
he'd leave. We remained close to each other,
with a small, nervous fear of hearing the door
open. You didn't dare let your kisses linger.
I wanted to be pretty and chose dresses you
might like. When we came down the stairs,
your classmates looked at me and glanced at
you with compliments in their eyes. I was
amused. It was puerile. You were happy.

Love, play, loyal affection... indeed, these
are all the things I have not stopped feeling for you since that time. Why do you ask
about "rediscovering" them? You stopped seeing them, because it was necessary for you to
no longer see them, since you were detaching

yourself from me. Now that you are settled once again… but elsewhere, you can, without danger to your new love, without indicting the opinion you have of yourself, ask me to appear to you as the woman from the time when you loved me. You do not use the word *love* anymore; it's *friendship* you say; but this new word covers the same things; it is indeed love you ask for, but a love that would be satisfied with its own existence, that would be nothing but kindness and renunciation.

Yet for such a long time you asked my heart to give you a complete love that gives and takes, a love of the spirit, a love of the body… that it seems difficult for me to brush away these tendencies, these desires that I acquired, that I loved, that I wanted. You want only kindness now; do you think that negating the rest is enough for it to no longer exist?

To appear in your eyes as the sublime woman you remember without guilt and without regret, I am to preserve this love for you and expect a few small favors you will kindly perform when you have nothing else to do. These small favors that I could have asked of others, that I could have not asked of you, if only my laziness had not inspired me to turn to you, these small favors are indeed the only gestures with which, for a long time now, you have manifested your devotion to me. And I did hesitate asking you them and sometimes regretted mentioning them at all. I perceived your bad mood and your refusal, if my request might in any way upset the daily arrangement of your habits; you did something for me when the thing to be accomplished could be carried out at the same time as those that fell into the order of your life. You would be more attentive today, to prove your friendship to me. I have not forgotten your "should the occasion arise…" But these things are not the marks of friendship to me. Those reside in the simple fact that there is someone to whom, at any moment, I can speak my thoughts, someone who will feel my joy or my troubles as I do. I do not believe that I can abuse; it seems to me that I can be selfish. What I require of a friend is to be able to ask a lot without fear of ever displeasing. That kind of friendship you have not given me for a long time.

And that is why I will not keep "this little place in my heart" for you. Out of a certain lover's puerility, I had promised you that I would always retain a small particle of true love for you, even if I loved passionately elsewhere. I am not the one getting married; within me is your image, taking up all the room; for me not to suffer anymore, you have to leave, so that one day, when it is uttered in front of me, your name will blow by me without touching a thing. I want this erasure, because I need peace; you—you have happiness; a little bit of love from me would not bring you anything.

Yes, it's very late; I have just turned off the lamp to let the light of the night come into my bedroom.

I feel warm and supple beneath the sheets, beneath the furs; the window is open wide to the 20-degree cold.

The snow outside is very white; and the muffled silence of snow reigns, that silence that awaits a revelation of which you know only that the thought of its arrival makes the heart beat more cheerfully. Outside the open windows, the incessant coughs that break up the night rise up; in the corridors, other coughs resonate. Coughs, always coughs, fly off into the frozen night. There's the cough of the young woman no one ever sees: all night long, tirelessly, ceaselessly, this cough crackles like dry wood; how many more days will we hear it before it is extinguished? The body is not exhausted enough for this to be the night when the glimmer of dawn carries it away. From the bedroom of the boy who, not long ago, left us quickly while hiding the blood that filtered through his lips, comes a deep and moist cough: every hiccup brings up blood… When will we be granted the relief of knowing the blood no longer flows? My neighbor lets her reassuring little cough be heard: I am not the only one keeping vigil. I too cough in response to test the state of my lungs. Will I feel that hollow, that pierced-bellows emptiness? Or the little rift that makes it seem as if a shred has become detached? Or else the full resonance that creates the illusion everything is mended? So many coughs in the night! Is it a hymn? Where is it going?

I am alone, but not more alone today; less, perhaps. Tonight, I know that everything is broken, and it is almost a relief. I will be able to react without being stopped by the depressing hope that things will return to what they were. I want to forget and to continue moving forward without looking toward you. The past wants to die. For several long months now, without knowing, I have been fighting for it not to die. I have clung to it, to you... with rage, with sadness, with love. I wanted everything to continue, unchanging... and every day I said: tomorrow, things will be like they were before. But "tomorrow" didn't come. Just yesterday, I was waiting for it: today I don't have to wait anymore. I should be more alone; I feel dizzy with the emptiness in which my love-deprived heart feels faint at the thought of the hollow days to come. You are gone, but I am finding myself again, and I am less alone than I was during the days when I was looking for you. I have come back to myself, and with myself, I will fight to carry on.

I know that "your old friendship" is disinterested and that I will perhaps need it some day. But I no longer think about it. Remain quietly in your happiness, and don't worry about me. Your mind this evening cannot hear the coughs rising louder and louder into the cold night. When you happen upon a funeral in Paris, you take off your hat; here, we hide; we may wish to look away when passing the cemetery. Tomorrow perhaps, as we try to laugh and to dance, we may hear the distant sound of a dying person being mourned. This one is dying from my illness; one day or another, why would I escape the same fate? Huddled together in this corner of the world, we can ask ourselves: "Whose turn next?" We can feel here, in the futility of days in which everyone is fighting with their dying breaths to escape their distress, all of human misery crying: "Why? Why?"

If I managed to make you feel this misery, you would hasten to forget it; and to reassure yourself, you would say what any man in good health says about places where people suffer: it's not as terrible as they say. I will not say anything to you. But leave me: you cannot be with me anymore. Leave me to suffer, leave me to be cured, leave me alone. Do not think that offering me friendship to replace love may be a balm for me; it may be when I am no longer in pain. But I am in pain; and when in pain, I withdraw without turning back. Do not ask me to look over my shoulder at you, and do not accompany me from afar. Leave me.

24 December, 1930

I knew I would receive a letter from you today, just as I know I will receive another one in eight days with your wishes for a happy new year. I crumpled up your letter and put it in the waste-paper basket. I felt a great relief.

Yet I can't say anything against it; I should write to you, thank you, and affirm my friendship in response to yours: I cannot. Your letter is very beautiful; my attitude will perhaps appear petty... but no letter could hurt me more, none could make me react more violently to pull away from you.

I will not write to you, because I want to forget you. Every envelope bearing your handwriting would be a torment for me; every sentence I would have to write, a battle; I would only be able to offer you platitudes, and my love would sting at this reminder of the past; I would try to understand your life, and it would cause me pain: I don't want to.

I will not write to you, because the way you let events unfold offended me. It is not your marriage that I find insulting. I thought I was more intimate a friend to you than a man, than a mistress, than a wife. It seemed to me that our affection was rare enough that it could accommodate a complete and gradual confession about the evolution of another love in your soul. But you acted like everyone else. You sought out my faults and now spoke only of them; did you need to reassure yourself that you were right to no longer love me? And you decided on your marriage, and you informed me of it; so to tell me this piece of news, you forgot my faults in favor of remembering my good qualities, that you could beg me to keep loving you. But as you well know, having so often repeated it to me over the last few months, I am, by nature, since the beginning of time, fundamentally selfish, and I'm bad-tempered: there's no point in showing myself to be otherwise in your eyes. For me, for me alone, it is better to make a clean break in our relationship: you can no longer offer me anything I desire right now.

And this morning's letter was precisely the one I needed to receive. I'd had a tendency to forget the pain I was feeling; I wanted to "turn it around"; my love imagined subterfuges to delude and satisfy itself, by willingly closing its eyes, with the bonds of affection that linger after any broken love. One still awaits a letter; one hopes, during a visit, to relive an illusion from the past; the heart beats when the door opens; the handshake produces the emotion of kisses past; one carefully keeps a rose that was brought; a banal compliment sounds like a confession of regret. Then the spell disappears, and one knows full well that it's all false. These are supple creeping vines that cling, that retain you in a vanished past and leave you without the strength to act and live.

If I didn't love you, I could see you again; when I no longer love you, I may see you again; at this moment I don't want to.

I don't want your words of love that are no longer that. I don't want to be lulled to sleep by your tender voice tonight because you have hurt me. If you try to hold onto a cat you have hurt, it scratches and runs away; do not try to hold onto me.

I don't like your solicitous words, I don't like your good wishes, I don't like that you imagine me unhappy and that a few words in a letter will fervently attempt to prove that you understand my pain and therefore feel close to me. You don't know anymore what it is to be close to me. I smiled at your "affection"; before my eyes the image of "Baby" appeared with an expression of rage and suffering: it was back when you loved me and when I had told you that I felt a lot of affection for you. You wish for me to be happy, and I can well imagine you trying to find me a husband, a lover to console me.

You think Christmas will be sad for me and you would like to cradle me in your arms. Oh! no, I don't want your caresses, and Christmas will only be sad if I want it to be. I crumpled up your letter, and I saw this as a deliverance. With a gesture, I shook off your caresses and my somnambulent slide into the past. I found that I was once again aggressive, prepared to look bravely at life without you; it is perhaps more beautiful without you: it is new... what will be written in it will always be the same thing; it will not be better... it will still be waiting. But what would be the point of me being near you and continuing the simulacra of a life that has been extinguished? That would be religion without faith; I need another faith: your presence would keep me from finding it. I am going to be merry; you won't have to console me. Christmas!

There was a dance tonight. The dining room was decorated in brightly colored streamers. A large table adorned with flowers gathered the sick, grouped as well as possible into couples according to external affinities. We danced very late into the night. I had fun. I had the feeling that a touch of my madness, of my past caprice, was returning to me. I observed my own behavior; I anticipated the possible consequences of a normal life... but I was acting. Who knows, maybe there's been a truce with the illness! Surely it must rest from

time to time, take Sundays and holidays…
On those days, it should be possible to live
as before. Tomorrow we'll resume the severe
life of the sick: we will have to fight. But
tonight it is good to laugh very loudly, while
the slight fear that you will feel your lungs
explode astonishingly vanishes; it is good to
drink the champagne that sets your cheeks
on fire; it's a touch of congestion, but let's not
think about that: there can be no hemop-
tysis tonight. And how good it is to dance!
You're able to remain on your feet, stand up,
sit down vivaciously. Your body rediscovers,
with near-religious happiness, the soft arch
for leaning into a partner, the intelligent
abandon that marries itself to the movements
of the other body and follows them, faithful
as a shadow and just as light. When the body
moves to a rhythm, another life emerges; the
world transforms to center itself on this very
place, in the middle of the chest, where the
sonorous rhythms of the instruments and the
supple oscillations of the ankles seem to con-
verge.

Dancing is life's happiest rhythm; dancing
when you believed you no longer could is a

victory. Lightly intoxicated by this rhythm, accompanied by my partner for the night, who by tomorrow will have forgotten this late evening, I slowly mounted the stairs to my door; and we took leave of each other after a kiss, without saying anything.

FROM THE PLAIN TO THE MOUNTAIN:
AN ESSAY BY JEAN MOUTON[1]

Commentary belongs to the category of "intimate writings." Jean Giraudoux, in a preface to the re-issue of Gerard de Nerval's *Aurélia*, expressed his astonishment at their rarity in French literature: "They presuppose one indispensable element: the intimacy of the writer with himself, and that is a relationship that the majority of our writers have avoided." These texts bring together great sin-

---

1. This essay first appeared in the 1986 French edition of *Commentaire*.

cerity with great lucidity, a union that occurs only on very rare occasions.

Three editions of *Commentary* were issued in quick succession: the first in 1933; the second in 1934 (preceded by a foreword by Charles Du Bos) from Rene-Louis Doyon's La Connaissance; the third, at the initiative of Jacques Chardonne, in 1936 (from Stock)[2]. The book was forgotten during the post-War years, when voluntarist and constructed literature prevailed. But fairly quickly, it attracted the attention of astute readers, especially women: In her memoirs (*Le Bruit de nos pas*, Volume IV p. 283) Clara Malraux affirmed: "*Commentary* should have been a milestone in women's literature. The first book written by a woman that is not about submission... Ah! She would not, like Collete, find it normal to accept unbidden caresses... A book of a sober sadness, written in the face of death and in the face of the masculine weakness that claims authority for itself; book of dignity, because one cannot prevent the departure of

---

2. In addition, an illustrated pirated edition appeared in Brussels in 1943 (éditions de La Mappemonde) and a German translation appeared in Berlin in 1934 (B. Ulrich Riemerschmidt).

the other, of the self. All this with a rather dry rigor. Admirable."

And, following that, Clara Malraux recounts how on the way home from a trip to China with André Malraux, in their reserved sleeping-car, an argument arose between them on the subject of *Commentary*: "'What is it you're reading with so much interest?' 'Be patient, I'll give it to you as soon as I've finished.' There was not much to do on this train but read or argue. We argued as soon as he had flipped through *Commentary*. 'Evidently, this book was made for your satisfaction.' 'Why?' 'Because it's a book of judgment.' 'To look with lucidity on a man should be forbidden to women when the inverse is not true, and men, since the beginning of time, have not been deprived of it?'"

Henri Gouhier, who visited Marcelle Sauvageot a few days before her departure for Davos, wrote in the December, 1933 edition of *Vie Intellectuelle*: "An irony without malice or metaphysical pretention sheds a soft light on this devastated landscape, an irony that seems to be less a disposition of the mind than a quality in things."

Commentary, written outside the margins of time, seized upon by vastly different beings, opposites in every way; one of them, Robert Brasillach, met a tragic fate. He was the first, in the spring of 1933, to appreciate "this book, rare and pure, almost miraculous for our time."[3] He added: "The more one re-reads it, the more true one finds it, and the more satisfying for the mind and for the heart… For the same emotions and the same impression of lucidity formed by suffering, sickness, and absence, I know of nothing else comparable save the final pages of Katherine Mansfield's journals, in which she writes of her husband and her life."

Jacques de Bouron Busset, following a visit to Hauteville, where Marcelle Sauvageot had gone for treatment, noted in his *Journal III (L'amour durable)*, "On the road between Salernes and Divonne, we pass le

---

3. *La semaine des quatre jeudis. (Four Thursdays.)*

Bugey and make a detour to see Hauteville[4], former tuberculosis capital and the setting for *Commentary*, the short narrative by Marcelle Sauvageot, preface by Charles Du Bos, which deserves an entire aisle in the library."

It was a brilliant era, following directly on World War I, in which the pursuit of liberty at all costs dominated. That meant above all to become oneself, rather than to collectively participate in predetermined transgressions, with no precise goal and essentially uniform outcomes. Some discovered this freedom dancing at all hours of the day and the night; others became initiates of Freudianism and transformed it into surrealism. It was at this moment that I met Marcelle Sauvageot, as a fellow student; and I was a witness to her life, often at distant intervals, until her death in Davos.

She was there to be treated for tuberculosis, which she had contracted several years earlier. She truly "lived her death," as Rainer Maria Rilke himself had hoped to do. Close

4. Marcelle Sauvageot's first visit to a sanatorium, October 1930 to June 1931.

to several writers of the surrealist movement, she had remained nonetheless profoundly attached to the search for the truth, casting aside all that seemed to her to be artificial, too literary, in particular Nathanaël's desire to "die without hope"—all the more so, as she had been on the brink of this despair. Fortuitous circumstances allowed for many friends to be with her during the final days of her life. Two of them were also living in Davos, in neighboring sanatoriums, being treated for the same disease: René Crevel, with whom she had a longstanding connection, and Jean Peltier, who later became a doctor of phthisiology in Rouen, and died in 1974.

Other friends came to Davos to see her, making a journey from the plain to the mountain of the sort that Thoman Mann, in *The Magic Mountain*, had provided a celebrated example. First, Henri Rambaud. He had expressed his admiration for *Commentary* in an article in the September 1, 1933 edition of the *N.R.F.*: "In the absence of the inventive powers a novel would have required, this beautiful book shines with an extraordinarily pure psychology of convention, all but ignor-

ing any trepidation about its brutality." He
had persuaded Charles Du Bos to write a
preface intended for a second edition of the
book. Charles Du Bos immediately felt the
same admiration as he did; he agreed to write
a foreword. What's more, having learned that
Marcelle Sauvageot was dying, he decided
to go see her in Davos and requested that
I accompany him. She was a stranger to
him, but he heard, without it having been
expressed, an appeal from which it seemed
impossible to extract himself. We arrived in
Davos on the first of January, 1934, where
we found Henri Rambaud, who had come to
speak to the patient (in no doubt that this was
her absolute end) about a plan for re-publica-
tion with La Connaissance. In the few days
that preceded the death of Marcelle Sauvageot, Charles Du Bos held several inerviews
with her; and a confluence between them was
immediately established. She entered into a
great peace, in which she must have gone to
sleep. As for Charles Du Bos, he was able to
write later in his journal, "Davos: one of the
culminating moments of my life."[5]

5. *Journal*, Volume IX, pp. 21-22, La Colombe, 1961.

FOREWORD TO THE SECOND EDITION
BY CHARLES DU BOS

To comment, says Littré, means to properly meditate and is etymologically linked to *'mens'*—a term ennobled in *De Trinitate,* and which represents the core of Saint Augustine's speculations: *sine mette,* he affirms, man is just a *bellua videns*, a "beast that sees." But there is no commentary of value that is not founded, at every instant, on reflection, the same that was defined by Leibniz: "Reflection is nothing but attention to what is within us." Marcelle Sauvageot possesses this focus on what is within her innately, and puts it in practice with a simplicity that in her hands seems to be the very *nature* of rigor. If the intelligence is feminine, in the positive sense in which a womanly quality augments the immediacy and delicacy of an intuitive grasp, its employment is masculine for its total absence of complacency. This is where lies the *distinction* of a book that restores to its title its original purity, and that is free from those "commentaries" with which almost all women (and men are women in this regard!), like protective bandages, envelop, attenuate and tone down their confessions.

"I would talk to myself, but the austerity of the monologue wore me out sometimes; it is so much easier to have an accomplice who sympathizes, approves, listens; you gain in importance; the things you say become tangible, form a novelistic universe in which you assume a role. To what extent do you respect the absolute truth?" I imagine that, even in the presence, in actual dialogue with this "accomplice," who, a few lines later and in terms much more accurate, she calls the "double": "I needed a double," Marcelle Sauvageot must hardly have strayed from "absolute truth." But the book does not begin until the actual dialogue is first interrupted by a separation in space, then broken by the arrival of the letter where the interlocutor announces his marriage, accompanying the news, with the quasi-inevitable masculine indelicacy of these cases, with the offer of his "friendship." But Marcelle Sauvageot knows what friendship is, even if the interlocutor does not: "Friendship, I believe, is a stronger and more exclusive form of love... but less 'showy.'" And there is nothing less 'showy' than *Commentary*, except perhaps the author as she is here revealed. Thus, Marcelle Sauvageot is brought back to her true nature as monologist: she quickly recognizes and even champions an eventuality that she had planned for, and that had even influenced, in advance, her way of being; and *Commentary* is a monologue in which the epistolary does not exceed—to borrow the title of a German book that had its moment of renown—*Briefe die ihn nicht erreichten*, "letters that never reached the addressee." In fact, as soon as the addressee ceases to be "Baby," who is described to us by his individual attributes, he becomes an anonymous character, Man himself, with his insufficiencies in love, with his duplicity, so instinctive, so organic it never rises to the level of consciousness: Marcelle Sauvageot's simplicity and rigor wouldn't want to, nor could they, continue their dialogue with him, and the interlocutor in *Commentary* is only the occasional cause thanks to which, once returned to her steady state, she renews the habit of "talking to herself," to herself alone, and brings the "austerity" of her monologue to its limit. There is no more suitable epithet than *austere* to characterize not only the content but also the artistic beauty of a book that resembles those statues in Japanese Early Art in which personal emotion is repressed and even the *expression* is that of immobile concentration.

"And when I am cured, you'll see how everything will be fine. I like speaking familiarly to you now that you're no longer here. I'm not accustomed to it, it feels forbidden to me: it's marvelous. Do you think one day I will really be able to speak to you this way? When I am cured, you will no longer find me bad-tempered. I am sick. You told me the sick force themselves to be sweeter to those around them: and you cited some beautiful examples for me. I do not love you when you are delivering sermons; you make me want to yawn, and if you reproach me, it means you love me less: you're comparing me to others. The sick are sweet, but what I am is exhausted; carrying on and saying "thank you" to those who do not understand is wearing away all my strength. But you, what would you have needed a "thank you" for? You didn't understand because you don't know. I asked you what kind of mood you'd be in if, for a mere eight days, you were unable to sleep. In reply you said such things never happen to you, but that it had to be unpleasant. Of course, you don't understand."

Of course: for a healthy person to understand a sick person requires something close to genius, just as for a sick person to always be sweet to those in good health requires something close to sainthood. No spatial separation equals the frontier drawn between people by sickness and health; and it is on the train that brings her to the sanatorium, that is thereby creating spatial separation, that the sick person formulates her protest. On the other hand, all women will recognize themselves in this universally feminine argument: "[I]f you reproach me, it means you love me less: you're comparing me to others." If women resort to this argument with a desperate and exasperating monotony, it is because, applied to men, it is all too often valid: all too often, if not when he "reproaches," at least when he "compares to others," it is indeed the sign that a man "loves less"—whereas "reproaching," "comparing to others" often results in a woman loving more because, relieved by the reproaches and comparisons, she subsequently feels she has made a stab at love, made a stab at *his* love, he who, in her eyes, is the embodiment of love. A common theme, but Marcelle Sauvageot weaves onto its fundamental melody the most subtle dissonant variation, because for her, in any given situation, there remains "a little corner of consciousness that is always aware of what is happening," that "does not stir," that "judges" and "measures":

"To be turned upside down and no longer know anything—that is happiness. But to hang on to a little corner of consciousness that is always aware of what is happening and that, because it is aware, can allow the intellectual and rational being to also enjoy, fully, with each passing second, something of the happiness that arises—to hang on to this little corner of consciousness that appreciates the slow evolution of joy, that follows it to its farthest reaches, isn't that happiness? There's a little corner that does not stir, but that remains witness to the joy being felt; that remembers and can say: I was happy, and I know why. I don't mind losing my head, but I want to capture the moment when I lose it, to push my understanding of my abdicating consciousness as far as it can go. We must not be absent from our own happiness."

Marcelle Sauvageot does not remain absent from any of her internal states; how precious and rare is it today to encounter such a respect for happiness, such a desire that, embalmed in memory's care, survives exactly the way it was lived. Let us remember the confession of François, hero of *Aimée*, who resembled Jacques Rivière like a brother: "Exempt of all vices, I was still afflicted by a perversion of a psychological nature. I had no love for happiness." It is because she loves both happiness and the memory of it, because she needs a "witness to the joy that was felt" that Marcelle Sauvageot is grateful for the "little corner that does not stir." Nothing escapes this "little corner," especially nothing that has to do with the other, when the other is the man one loves; and, whether or not the "little corner" wants it this way, not stirring gives it the most ruthless advantage over the other: "This corner of myself judged you, measured you; and in judging and measuring you I saw your weaknesses, your insufficiencies." Here is where Marcelle Sauvageot's subtle, dissonant variation intervenes: for most women, the knowledge of the loved man's "insufficiencies" represents the *weak moment* of love that will only become *strong* again afterward, in the reaction against the attack knowledge has made on love; knowledge and love put themselves in play according to a rhythm of quick and constantly self-renewing succession; Marcelle Sauvageot, on the contrary, allows for knowledge and love to coexist in perfect simultaneity; this is why she adds:

"[W]here is the harm in my staying, in my accepting these insufficiencies, in my loving them? O, Man! You always want to be admired. You do not judge, you do not measure the woman you love. You are there, you take her; you take your happiness, she seems not to belong to herself anymore, to have lost all sense of anything: you are happy. To you she cried: I love you, and you are satisfied. You are not brutal; you are gentle, you talk to her, you worry about her; you comfort her with tender words; you cradle her in your arms. But you do not judge her, since you are asking her to be happy through you and to tell you that she is happy through you. But if you notice two eyes watching you, then smiling, you revolt. You feel that you have been "seen" and you don't want to be seen: you want only 'to be.' […] [Y]our weaknesses are my own. I discovered them little by little, by examining you without rest. I suffer from these faults of yours, but I wouldn't want you to change. […] Nothing is more endearing than weaknesses and faults: it is through them that one penetrates the beloved's soul, a soul perpetually concealed by the desire to seem like everybody else. […] Do not complain that I am judging you and measuring you: I know you better, and that is not to love you less."

What Marcelle Sauvageot is defining here, what she herself feels, and for which there is almost no single example of life granting reciprocity to one who feels it, is nothing less than a *knowing love*, that which for ten years Goethe and Charlotte von Stein tasted, experiencing its cutting edge, reproduced in the verse play that is unique in all of poetry: *Warum gabs du uns die tie fen Blicke*, a love about which I wrote in one of my unpublished *Aperçus* on Goethe: "To love one another, not without knowledge but, on the contrary, by knowing the other—and here we must even add to love each other *because* we know each other, since knowing is the foundation, the core of love—to love because each sees the other as he is and not as he never was—ah! here is one of the rarest, most supreme human masterpieces."

But, since it is reciprocal, *knowing love* postulates above all equality between beings, and I leave to the readers of *Commentary*, by way of its piercing analyses, so serene in their disenchantment, the pleasure of discovering in what consists, here, the irreducible power difference. And there is more: a crucial sentence shows, and this is Marcelle Sauvageot's last resort on the sentimental level, that there is a strictly creative love which, from the moment of true, reciprocal comprehension creates a third being out of the others' union: a being at the same time alive and immaterial, present and invisible, made from the "best" of both; a best that exists at its authentic form in each, and that they *want* to lead to its perfect culmination—the love that Robert and Elizabeth Browning create, and out of which Browning's *By the Fireside* unravels the inexhaustible and forever ascending metamorphoses. Here is Marcelle Sauvageot's sentence: "And what hurts me is not so much the death of a love as that of a truly living being that the two of us created, that perhaps I created alone… This being was a union of you and me, as we wanted ourselves to be." There is nothing humanly above the creation that unfolds from love, and this is why the subtitle of the book I plan to write on Robert and Elizabeth Browing bears the subtitle, "or the fullness of human love."

"That perhaps I created alone." Alone, Marcelle Sauvageot created this "truly living being;" once love is dead, she is left to her essential solitude:

"I tried to hold onto a small support separate from you, so I could cling to it the day you would no longer love me. This small support was not another man, it was not a dream, nor an image. It was what you called my egoism and my pride; it was my self that, in my suffering, I wanted to be able to find again. I wanted to be able to hold myself tight, alone with my pain, my doubts, my lack of faith. When I am in distress, only my sense of self gives me the strength to go on. When everything is changing, when everything is hurting me, I am me with myself. To have lost myself, I would have had to be sure I no longer needed myself."

Let us allow an outdated "accomplice," like many others have, the right to equate "egoism" and "pride" with the movement—instinctive and elemental in the manner of a need, and at the same time concentrated in the being's entire dignity—that consists in "holding oneself to oneself." No movement is deeper, more poignant, more inevitable; none can, as an initiating movement, develop more consequences. Let us remember Maine de Biran's true statement: "Two poles of social sciences: the person *me*, from which everything starts, the person *God*, where it all ends." Whether it all ends at *God* or not, it is clear that attentive and reflective selves can only come to their end from *me*, and it is from *me* that it all starts. That the heart's suffering and the body's sickness find themselves transplanted onto the innateness of reflective attention— ah! only those who "do not, *of course*, understand" either one can foist the labels "egoism" and "pride" onto this withdrawal of all the energy on the citadel.

But what happens inside the citadel? Is it the monologue that begins and continues? the inner dialogue that is introduced? "I talked to myself," but there are two ways of talking to oneself: there is the pure monologist's approach, of which Amiel is the limiting case, the same Amiel of whom I once wrote: "He knows himself from this limitless, detached, inhuman understanding, where you can see yourself, so to speak, walk in front of yourself a second time, always the same and always predictable": the peril lies in this cyclical and circular nature, as Ramon Fernandez said of Proust's *Intermittences of the Heart*, "To progress is only to understand more and more that one does not progress"—, and there is also Augustine's, from the thirty-third year, as expressed in the first letter to Nébride: "I read your letter by my glimmering lamp after my supper. I was close to going to bed—I do not say sleep because once in bed, I thought for a long time and spoke to myself, Augustine with Augustine." "Augustine with Augustine": this is how a true inner dialogue begins. If everything starts from *me*, if it is into *me* that everything must first withdraw, then the next stage relies on the splitting of *me*— oh! not the splitting that psychologists have familiarized us with, not even the one Valéry wrote about in a recent commentary on *Note and Digression* and on his *Léonard*: "Personality is composed of memories, habits, penchants, reactions. It is, all in all, the whole of the being's most immediate responses—even when this immediacy brings with it a tendency to defer. Now, all this may seem accidental when compared to that pure and simple consciousness whose unique function is *to be*. It is, on the contrary, completely *impersonal*"—, but is rather this *spiritual* splitting in which, beyond the *psychological* and *impersonal* zones, in the inner dialogue of the two Augustines, one of them, the Augustine whose *me* lives in concrete time, discovers that the other Augustine bursts past and transcends him, is totally incommensurable with him, and that this other is no less than *Augustine's soul*, a soul not at all *impersonal* but *personal* to the point of uniqueness, *internum oeternum*, an inner reality that, for us, is eternal—, and this is why, in *De Anima et ejus origin,* in the tract *Of the Soul and its Origin*, Augustine offers, in the sixty-fifth year, a sentence the truth of which has not been exhausted: "Too high, too powerful for ourselves, we cross the narrow boundaries of our science, cannot get a hold of ourselves but yet, we are never outside of ourselves."—"We cannot get a hold of ourselves", —and here lie the gravest misinterpretation and the most recurrent error—not because this "us" is "accidental compared to" a "perfectly impersonal" consciousness, nor because in is inconsistency this "me" veers toward emptiness or nothingness, but the opposite, because "too high, too powerful for ourselves, we cross the narrow boundaries of our science." Jacques Rivière knew it when he said, during one of his more penetrating intuitions: "There is always a subtle, discouraging difference between us and our soul." The real end of the inner dialogue is to lead us to this mysterious threshold where, without "getting a hold of" it, we come upon our very soul; and to have come upon it is enough for us to never be able to doubt its existence again. "Faith in the soul," I have written elsewhere, "is a reality, just like the soul itself: it is the same reality, a reality in which we can live while we await to be led to the full reality for which our faith in the soul destines us," and sooner or later we will be led there, because grace never refuses itself to those who do not refuse to go all the way to their soul, and sooner or later, the soul will erase itself in front of God, its creator, and on that day, in the Saint Augustine of the *Confessions*, the soul addresses God, for all intents and purposes, with the *cry of recognition: Tu autem eras interior intimo meo.* "But you were more within me than my most intimate source."

This is the same trajectory that is offered to all who are *innately attentive*, that opens a path before them guaranteeing the most prolific and elevated use of their abilities: it is proffered to all of them equally, the sick and the well: and yet, the well ones, even if they are innately attentive, are prone to innumerable distractions, and often, as a result, sickness is not the only thing they "do not, of course, understand." If they are already innately attentive, the sick are additionally *invitees to attention*—as they are named by Claudel in an admirable text with the same title:

"If I could choose, I would address myself not to those whose sickness is just an accident, a momentary test, but, to speak cruelly, to those for whom it is a *vocation*, a permanent and complete change of nature. I speak, as Pascal, to the *acclimated*, to the patients who do not await their recovery but, having accepted their fate, take a lucid view, both Christian and wise, of their condition, and who are capable of meditating on this weighty expression: "My hope is in my attention."

Attentive by *vocation*, and "invited to attention" by this other vocation that sickness has given her, how could Marcelle Sauvageot's "hope" *not* be "in" her "attention," how could she not reencounter the One referred to in Claudel's verse:

Someone in me who is more myself than am I.

Christmas Vigil—28 December, 1933

NOTE BY CHARLES DU BOS
14 JANUARY, 1934

The preceding pages left for their destination in Davos on December 29th. I knew Marcelle Sauvageot's state did not allow her to write and I had set out to be by her side: first, because I did not want to put out this Foreword before it had been approved, before she could tell me it contained nothing that she found inexact or wished to be different; second, and most important, because I wanted to be there in the event that the end of this Foreword might awaken a desire for self-examination which she could now, in the fullness of her freedom, undertake amidst a friendly presence. I arrived in Davos in the afternoon on January 1st: as the double effort of reading on her own and being attentive to what she read had become impossible, I learned that the Foreword had been read to her the night before by a friend, at a moment when her lucidity—always perfect when she was not under the influence of narcotics—showed extreme vigilance. On the day of my arrival, I saw her with the two friends who were there with her, and the conversation, in which she and I met each other for the first time, limited itself to *Commentary* and the Foreword. It was the day after, at the end of the afternoon on January 2nd, that we had our first hour alone together; this hour was enough for her to tell me afterward: "At base, I don't know if I have really lost faith," after having listened again to the *Pater*, the *Ave* and the *Credo*, and added this sentence only: "I've recited these prayers often and have always subscribed to them." The next morning, in the same admirable spirit of simplicity and *childhood* (in the sense that *Saint Thérèse de l'Enfant Jésus* has restored for us), reconciled with God and enwrapped in a peace that would not leave her again, she received—and two of us with her—"the living bread from the sky," and the next morning, another friend had arrived to join us and so the four of us received it. As I was obligated to return to Paris, my last visit to her was on January 5th, and it was in Paris that, during the night of the 6th, the news that she had peacefully passed away at five in the afternoon reached me, while the bells called believers to salvation in honor of the Epiphany. As I had asked her, during our last conversation, who she thought had been able to portray the landscape of Lorraine that was so dear to her, and she had replied: "Claude, him only, in a few of his skies and backgrounds"—on Thursday, January 11th, in weather and light worthy of Claude, with the Coast of Hures in front of us and the spur of Eparges on our left, we brought her back to her church and to the cemetery in her village, Trésauvaux.

C.D.B.
14 January, 1934
Second weekend after the Epiphany

COLOPHON

This book was printed and bound in an edition of 1250 by McNaughton & Gunn in Saline, Michigan. The covers were printed letterpress by Sway Space in Brooklyn, New York. Typesetting and design are by goodutopian using Caslon and Futura.